This Little Tiger book
belongs to:

_____

_____

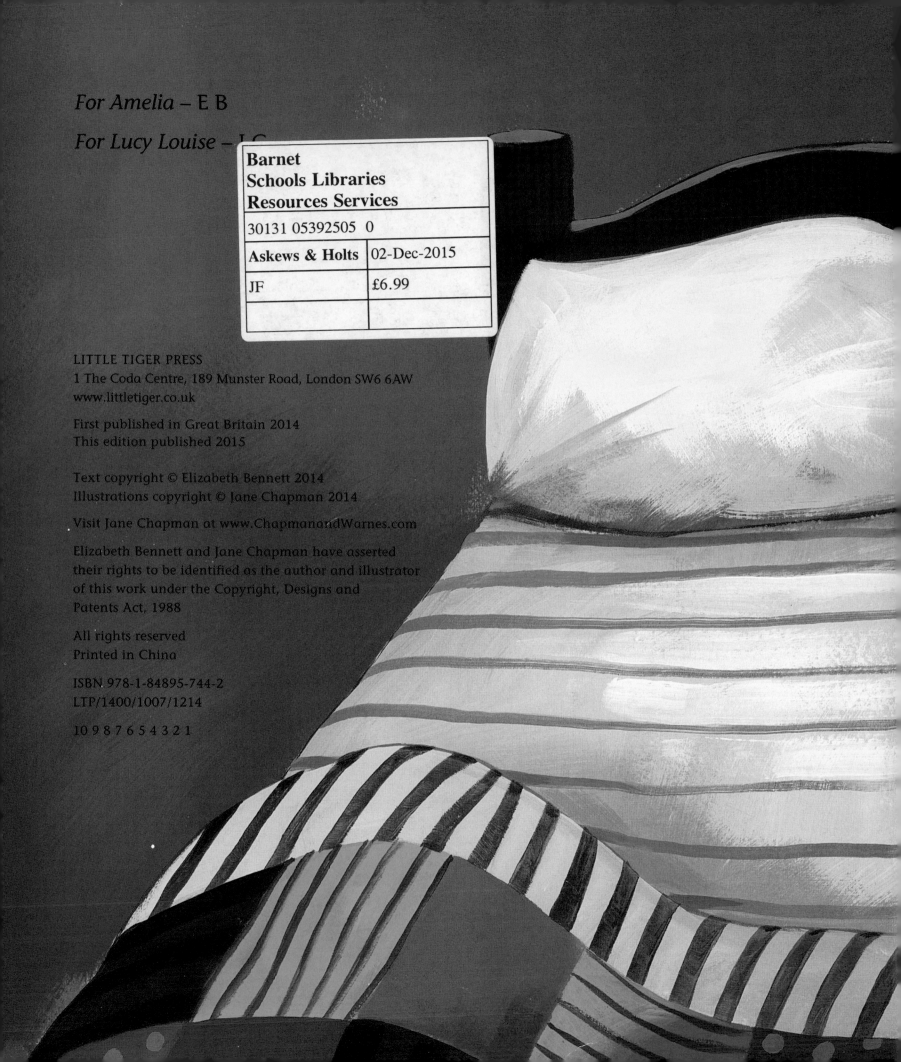

For Amelia – E B

For Lucy Louise – J C

LITTLE TIGER PRESS
1 The Coda Centre, 189 Munster Road, London SW6 6AW
www.littletiger.co.uk

First published in Great Britain 2014
This edition published 2015

Visit Jane Chapman at www.ChapmanandWarnes.com

ISBN 978-1-84895-744-2
LTP/1400/1007/1214

10 9 8 7 6 5 4 3 2 1

Elizabeth Bennett

Jane Chapman

Big

and Small

LITTLE TIGER PRESS
London

On a bright
and sunny day,
Big and Small
go out to play.

Big

climbs high.

Small crawls low.

When
suddenly,
Small stubs his toe.

They cross a stream.
Jump, skip, hop, hop.

When suddenly,
Small has to stop.
"A little help, please!"
calls Small.

What's for **lunch**? Hmmmmmm. Let's see . . .

...When suddenly,
Small spots a bee!
"A little help, please!"
calls Small.

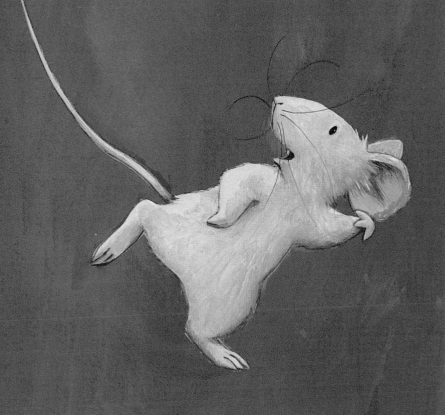

High on a

When **suddenly**,
Small's down
a hole.
"A little help, please!"
calls Small.

Back

home to bed.

They're warm
and snug.
But Big can't sleep —
he needs a hug.
"A little help, please!"
calls Big.

More **big** adventures for little ones!

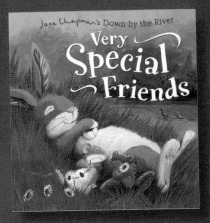

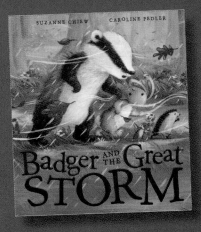

For information regarding any of the above titles or for our catalogue, please contact us:
Little Tiger Press, 1 The Coda Centre, 189 Munster Road, London SW6 6AW
Tel: 020 7385 6333 • Fax: 020 7385 7333 • E-mail: contact@littletiger.co.uk • www.littletiger.co.uk